CHAPTER 1

If the Queen were coming for tea and you made her a chocolate cake, I bet that you would try very hard to make sure that it was the loveliest cake she had ever tasted. I expect that you would be very careful to weigh out all the ingredients and follow the recipe to the best of your ability. In fact, I'm positive that you would not add anything horrid to the mixture, anything horrid like a jar of slug poo or a pot of worm snot. Slug poo and worm snot are two ingredients that chef's do not recommend.

But imagine if, when your back was turned, the jar of stinky, smelly slug poo or the pot of dirty, slimy worm snot fell into the cake mixture by accident? What would happen if you served it straight from the oven when it was warm and squidgey for Her Majesty the Queen of England? Well, you wouldn't know until it was too late would you? You wouldn't know until the poor Queen was being sick everywhere and her ladies in waiting were screaming at the tops of their voices. You wouldn't know until then, that the recipe you had been following so very carefully had turned into a recipe for disaster!

PROFESSOR MUDGETT

I suppose the same thing might happen if you were following a secret formula, just as Professor Mudgett was that fresh spring morning. He was being so careful to add the right amount of all the chemicals and compounds, that he didn't notice when he knocked over the cup of tea his daughter Sally had left for him. He didn't notice when the tea started to trickle into the metal pot that contained the secret recipe and he still didn't notice when little Sally did her best to clean up the mess around him.

SALLY MUDGETT

"If this special formula works," announced Professor Mudgett, "It will be my greatest triumph to date!"

"Have you had any other triumphs?" asked Sally, as she tidied the kitchen.

"Not yet, but you wait and see! If this does what I hope it will do, we will be rich! And you know what that means?"

"We will be able to buy back our lovely restaurant?'

"Yes Sally, we can buy back the restaurant and move out of this disgusting dump!"

Now when most people refer to their house as a dump or a rubbish tip, we get a picture in our minds of a messy, untidy home that needs a good clean. We don't expect them to actually live in the depths of a refuse centre! But the Mudgetts' house was right in the middle of the town dump and, although it was indeed a fresh spring morning, the stench of all that rubbish could make your nose spin.

Professor Mudgett thought about all this as his daughter peered wistfully into the pot of bubbling, frothing liquid.

"Don't worry, Sally" He reassured her, "I've been so careful adding all these scientific ingredients, I know nothing will go wrong."

But oh dear! If only he had known about the hot water, milk, two lumps of sugar and the teabag that were swirling around in that secret formula, he would not have been so confident.

Instead, the Professor beamed with satisfaction as a hot bubble burst from the metal pot, followed by a pale thin cloud.

"I think it's time!" the Professor whispered mysteriously. Delicately he removed the pan from the heat and onto the kitchen table.

"I can't quite believe it Sally." Her father continued in a low voice.

"All these months of hard work and it's finally here! The question is will it work?"

"What's it supposed to do, Dad?"

"Haven't I told you yet?" asked the Professor. His daughter shook her head.

"Well, I must have forgotten. But it's a very complicated thing to explain to a little girl like you."

"I'm sure you can do it. You're very good at explaining things normally. Especially thinks like, why I can't have any pocket money or why I have to go to bed early."

"That's very true," said the Professor, sitting down in preparation.

"Now Sally," he began.

"Imagine you were on the high seas in a tiny little sailing boat and, suddenly, a huge ocean liner came steaming across the waves and crashed into you. What do you think might happen?"

"The boat would be crushed and I'd sink to the bottom of the sea," Sally replied, somewhat horrified.

"Yes you're right. The boat would sink. But! If you had coated your tiny little sailing boat with my special formula and an ocean liner

came steaming towards you, something very different would happen. The minute that hulking brute of a ship touched the sides of your craft, it would bounce straight off! It would bounce so far that it would probably end up back in the docks. That's because this wonderful mixture will make anything and everything indestructible.

"I'm willing to bet that its fire proof! Hurricane proof! Bullet proof! Bombproof and even Elephant Proof!"

"Is it tea proof though?" Sally enquired, quietly.

"Tea proof? What a peculiar question Sally! But I can't wait to test it out! What can we use? Something that isn't very strong and is as light as a feather."

"A feather?" Sally said, presenting one plucked from the duster.

"Excellent choice Sally," laughed the Professor.

"Now prepare yourself for something amazing. Watch as I dip this ordinary feather in the special mixture."

Sally held her breath. Holding the feather with a pair of tongs, the Professor lowered it into the pot before lightly placing it on the table.

The limp, wet feather seemed to dry right before their eyes.

"This," began her father, "Is now the strongest feather on the planet.

"I'm going to prove this to you, by hurling it from the table. Now you must stand back as I need to use my full body weight to knock the feather onto the floor and it may break a few tiles on impact."

As he prepared himself mentally for the test, Sally darted forward to rescue the formula. 'Just in time' she thought as she watched her father launch himself off a chair and shoot across the kitchen table. The whole thing collapsed from underneath him and he landed head first on the tiles. The poor Professor sat up with a confused expression embedded on his face. Sally tried her best not to laugh.

"What happened to my amazingly strong feather?"

"It went up your nose," she giggled, helping her father get back on to his feet.

Professor Mudgett snorted with disgust and the feather floated gently to the ground.

"Why didn't it work Sally?" he moaned. "I just don't understand."

Sally wondered if she should tell her father about the cup of tea that had found it's way into the mixture. But before she could say anything, Professor Mudgett started to wail, "If only I still had my restaurant! I could spend all day experimenting with delicious ingredients instead of scientific powders and potions. What is the good of secret formula if it doesn't work?"

"It's not your fault Dad," His daughter ventured.

"Yes, it is my fault. Everything is my fault! I've let you down again! I'm sorry Sally!

"I don't mind losing everything but it's not fair on you. Why should you lose everything too?"

"I haven't lost everything" Sally said, "I've still got you, haven't I?"

"Well that's very true," said the Professor, cheering up a bit.

"And I've got the blue dragon. We didn't lose that did we?"

"That stupid thing," scoffed her father. "What a piece of old rubbish that is. No wonder that man didn't want it, though he took everything else we had..." Professor Mudgett continued in this way for quite some time and Sally, half listening, gazed out of the kitchen window into the garden beyond. In the middle of the dull dry patch of earth where nothing grew, sat a very odd looking object. It was a statue of a dragon and was painted in the brightest blue. The stone dragon was the only thing left of the restaurant they had once owned. It had a rather stumpy snout, and was in possession of a single ear. But Sally liked to imagine that, if those wings could unfurl from the small, stone body, how magnificent they would look.

"Are you listening to me, Sally?"

"Yes of course," replied the little girl turning back to look at her father.

THE BLUE DRAGON

"You were saying?"

"I was saying that I'm going to chuck the formula away, because it's worse then useless. Just like your old Dad."

"Don't say that," said Sally. "That's not true."

But it was a grim faced Professor who picked up the pot of formula and stormed into the garden. Now, although he was a grown man and had been walking upright for many years, he was still prone to stumbling and tripping over.

A tiny pebble was the culprit on this occasion, causing the poor Professor to lose his balance and throw the formula high into the air. Instead of the mixture going over beyond the Mudgett's garden, it hit the fence with an almighty splat! Not only that but a huge dollop now covered Sally's blue dragon statue.

Sally ran in for a cloth to wipe away the formula but, when she'd got back, it had dried as fast as it had done on the feather.

"Oh Dad, the dragon's covered in the mixture!"

"Don't worry," was her father's reply. "It won't do anything." And with that he marched back indoors, hands on hips.

"If only something would happen," sighed the little girl, as she tapped the dragon's wing. "What a change that would be."

Just then the heavens opened and a torrent of cold rain fell from the blackening sky.

"That's not what I meant!" Sally cried glaring up at the clouds.

Then she ran inside for cover.

21

The rain had stopped by morning. Sally awoke to hear a strange scuffling sound coming from the kitchen. When she heard the sound of pots crashing to the ground, Sally leapt out of bed and hurried downstairs. Professor Mudgett was waving a broom about and was extremely annoyed.

"Out! Out!" he shouted. "Morning Sally. I hope I didn't disturb you? Get Out!"

"You did actually. Who are you shouting at?"

But before she could ask any more important questions the Professor started running around the kitchen as though he was chasing something.

"Stop your pooping! Your dirty bird!" he cried.

Sally looked up. A rather scruffy looking feathered thing was fluttering above. It swooped down to settle on top of the fridge. Sally had never seen a bird like that before. It had a small fat beak and its brown feathers seemed to sprout out in all directions.

"Can you help me get this thing out Sally! It's leaving droppings all over the worktop."

"How did it get in Dad?" Sally queried as the bird flew past.

"In through the open window, probably," he answered, running to catch it.

But Sally knew that they would never leave a window open. Nor would anyone living in the middle of a rubbish dump.

The bird started to squawk.

"Is it a chicken or a crow, or both?" wondered the little girl.

"Let's just get it out before, it makes a mess on my breakfast," the Professor said, flinging the kitchen door open and shooing the bird out.

He followed the bizarre bird and watched as it flew sideways up into the sky.

Professor Mudgett was then met with a rather unexpected sight. In fact, it surprised him so much that his jaw dropped and he nearly toppled over.

"Sally?" he said.

"I'm here, Dad," replied a little voice behind him.

The pair gazed into the garden beyond.

What had once been a small dry patch of earth was now bursting with trees and plants!

SALLY MUDGETT
~ and the Blue Dragon ~

Out of the fence, sprouted, fruits and flowers in such abundance that Sally thought it looked more like a jungle then a garden.

On the branches sat a multitude of birds, twittering joyfully in their magical new oasis and the strange chicken-crow bird squawked excitedly, amongst them,

"What happened, Sally?" asked her bewildered father.

"I'm not sure. All I know is that yesterday you spilt the formula over the fence and now, we have a beautiful green forest growing out of it!"

"That's it! My formula!" cried Professor Mudgett "I can hardly believe it! This old wooden fence has been here for years, dry and dead, but now it's a living thing. A glorious woodland!"

Sally wandered around touching and smelling new leaves and flowers as real as her own two hands. No longer could she smell the stench of mouldy cabbage and clammy socks, but the fragrant aroma of flowers and ferns were filling her nostrils.

The Professor picked up the empty potion pot and hurried towards the house.

"I'm going to make some more of this stuff," he said. "It's not quite what I expected but what a wonderful result! Thank goodness it's only been spilt in the garden. Who knows what else it could bring to life!"

Sally's heart skipped a beat. She ran through the undergrowth searching frantically for the small stone dragon and what do you think she found? Nothing! To her horror the dragon had gone!

SALLY MUDGETT
~ and the Blue Dragon ~

THE BLUE DRAGON

CHAPTER 2

Now do you remember right at the beginning of the story we talked about chocolate cakes? We said that although something might be called a chocolate cake it might well be made of slug poo or indeed worm snot and not taste nearly as good. I suppose that if the new owner of the restaurant next to the Mudgett's house were a cake, he would be a cake made, not only from the smelliest slug poo, but also the slimiest worm snot.

His name was The Mighty King Poe. It was a silly name because he was neither mighty nor a king. It was an even sillier name when you consider that he used to be called Derek Scrunge.

Derek Scrunge is not a good name for someone whose ambition it is to be clever and evil. But I'm quite sure that Professor Mudgett would rather have lost his restaurant to a man called The Mighty King Poe then to a man called Derek Scrunge. So the Mighty King Poe it was. Now King Poe had two concerns in life. They were making money and looking after his big hairy moustache. He knew nothing about running a restaurant

KING POE
(*Derek Scrunge*)

or about Chinese cuisine. Perhaps his concerns should have been about the quality of his restaurant's food.

As one customer put it,
"These crispy pancakes taste just
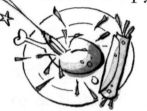
like cardboard and
the crispy duck
tastes like shredded
wheat and gravy!"

Well the trouble was,
that the pancakes *were*
cardboard and the
crispy duck *was*
shredded wheat and
gravy! The Mighty King Poe would
do anything to save money!

The night before, King Poe had
decided to go for a walk around the
rubbish tip for some new recipe
ideas. Although it was nearly dark,
he combed his big moustache and set
off towards the Mudgett's house. He
liked to go there and be reminded

just how silly that 'Mudgett man' was. Peering over their fence, he was rather disturbed to see that their garden looked a lot more like a garden then usual. Where did they get the money for all those plants? His eyes must be playing tricks. Perhaps he should invest in some glasses. When he was Derek Scrunge he would have worn a pair of glasses and would know for sure. But those days were gone. He couldn't quite put his finger on it, but something had definitely changed. While he pondered on this, a 'money making' idea hit him! Perhaps he could let customers eat their meals outside in a garden! This would mean that instead of clearing the table, he could throw all the contents over into the dump ready for the next customer. If only he could get a path cleared from the restaurant right into the Mudgett's garden! Hey presto! His customers could enjoy their disgusting meals in beautiful surroundings and he could charge them extra!

Perhaps he could think of a clever way to trick that man Mudgett into losing his garden too.

As The Mighty King Poe was planning to make the Mudgett's lives even more miserable, he felt something tickle his nose. Maybe it was his moustache blowing in the wind but it had been coated in so much hairspray that it couldn't move. No, what was tickling him was a thin green tendril of ivy growing right before his eyes. He looked about; the fence seemed to be moving! Young shoots were feeling their way up and creeping into the rubbish beyond. But the how's and why's of this miraculous sight did not really concern him. Not when there were pounds and pennies to be made. He would need to make a path right through  The Mudgett's garden and get rid of that unsightly lizard statue sat right in the middle. Picking up a bottle, The Mighty King Poe threw it hoping to smash the little stone dragon. It wobbled slightly as the bottle hit it. Funny, but it looked somehow different at night and it looked even more peculiar as it slowly turned around to glare at him! He dived back down behind the fence. "Don't be silly," he told himself. "It's made of stone and you are just imagining things." Taking a deep breath, The Mighty King Poe gingerly peeped at the dragon once more. There it was, an ugly blue statue. But just to make sure he thought it best to throw something else at it, something else like an old wheel perhaps. Thud! The wheel hit the stone dragon, knocking it onto its side. The Mighty King Poe scrambled up on top of

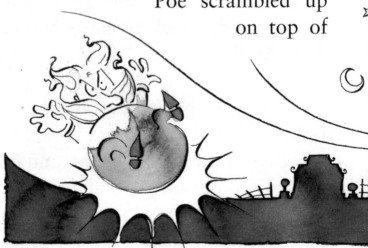

the fence to have a better look. But the dragon had gone! What was going on? Suddenly... whoosh! Something flew past him! Now it was his turn to wobble and fall to the ground. What in the world was that? It flew past him again and whatever it was, it was much bigger then a bat and much bigger then a bird! And it was breathing fire. Now what was bigger then a bat or a bird and could breathe fire?

He didn't know, but he could feel a rather strange sensation on his face. Now what was it? Hot! Burning! His beloved moustache was on fire! The Mighty King Poe slapped his face wildly and wished he hadn't used quite so much hairspray that day. As he did so, his attention was drawn to something perched on top of a stack of old cars. Blinking at him, sat a small blue dragon, its silhouette clearly outlined against the moon. Its eyes ablaze like small furnaces watching his every move. King Poe could not quite believe what he was seeing. Was he dreaming? He didn't know, but let me tell you how his brain worked! If you and I came face to face with a small blue dragon sitting on top of a pile of cars in the middle of a rubbish dump, we would think a great many things, but we would not be thinking about a business opportunity. While the creature eyed him suspiciously from its rusty roost, the fat man with the moustache was thinking about money! He was thinking that if he could get that small blue beastie into a cage and into his restaurant how many customers would come in and eat cardboard pancakes filled with shredded wheat in gravy just to get a look at that dragon. He must catch it! He dashed back into his restaurant to see what he could use to ensnare his prize. He found a broom and thought that he might knock the dragon from the pile of disused cars. Poor King Poe, he wasn't thinking!

The dragon was quite content to sit there and clean between his claws with a long forked tongue. The fat man returned armed with the broom ready for action. As The Mighty King Poe approached, it stopped what it was doing and glared at him. Just as the broom came close to knocking the small animal down, it breathed out a large plume of fire turning the broom to a pile of ash. Bored with this silly exercise the blue dragon launched itself into the air and glided back safely into the Mudgett's garden.

"What a beauty!" admired The Mighty King Poe as it flew overhead. "And what an attraction for my restaurant!" He climbed up onto the cars to see if he could spot the little monster. Unfortunately, he slipped off a car bonnet and hurtled to the ground. The last thing he remembered about that night was thinking, "Thank goodness my moustache cushioned the fall!"

The blue dragon hovered for a few seconds before landing at the side of the Mudgett's shed. Feeling a little tired and afraid, it was pleased to discover a small hole it could creep through for safety. Once inside, the tiny monster snuffled and snorted about, before nestling in amongst a pile of broken pots.

The air had turned colder by now and the little blue shape found itself shivering in the darkness. Luckily, dragons have a wonderful talent, which can be used to combat things like shivering and the dark. The dragon used this talent and produced a solid stream of fire, which travelled up the sides of the shed. As the small beastie delighted in its golden flames, neither Sally nor

Professor Mudgett stirred from their deep sleep. I suppose this was due to an extremely good mug of cocoa before bed. Outside in the garden, the temperature was rising and the Mudgett's shed was burning. Sensibly, our little blue friend inched out of its hiding place and snuggled up against the warm bricks of the Mudgett's house.

CHAPTER 3

Neither Mudgett had noticed that their shed had burnt down. They were too busy noticing the new garden that had sprung up, consuming everything in its path. Still searching for the little stone dragon, Sally tugged at the leaves and branches, hoping that it lay somewhere underneath. She pulled on a vine and just as it snapped off in her hand, another started to grow in its place, thicker and lusher then the last.

" Dad," she whispered. "I think that the fence is still growing!"

Professor Mudgett narrowed his eyes. "That special formula of mine may need some serious alterations, I certainly wouldn't have expected a sustained acceleration of growth."

"Dad, I think I should remind you that some of the formula fell on my blue dragon.

"And now I can't find it!"

"Well don't worry, it'll be around somewhere," he reassured. "But I think we should go inside before we find it too difficult to get out of this jungle."

Hacking their way through the garden, Sally and the Professor made it safely inside the house.

Something made them stop dead in their tracks. Something long and thin and blue disappeared up the staircase and into the bathroom.

Professor Mudgett held on to his daughter and whispered, "It looks like a snake. You stay here and I'll go up."

"I don't think so Dad," Sally whispered back. " That was a tail!"

" In that case, I'll stay here and you go up!" Professor Mudgett whimpered.

"We could call the police," Sally said. "Or we could go together and investigate."

Thinking that was their best option, Professor Mudgett and his daughter crept up the stairs following in the monsters paw prints.

The odd shaped creature had padded up the stairs a few minutes before. It was feeling a little out of sorts because a big fat man with a huge moustache had spent half the night trying to hit it with a broom. The little dragon had not had a drink since it had come into being and was very thirsty. It had headed into the bathroom because it could smell the water in the taps.

Outside the bathroom door, Professor Mudgett was preparing to go in and face the danger head on.

"You stay out here," He told Sally, " this could be dangerous, if it tries to eat me I want you to get help."

Sally rolled her eyes as her father opened the bathroom door as though it were a gateway into another world. After hearing him gasp, She marched in straight past him, ready to face anything. Now, although Professor Mudgett was a scientist with a big brain, he wasn't very good at facing dragons. He gazed fearfully into the mini monsters yellow eyes, then fainted. The dragon slumped up against the toilet cistern puffing in disgust. .

"Are you alright Dad?" She whispered.

" I'm not very good at being an adult, Sally."

" I know Dad, but luckily I'm very good at being a little girl."

"You'll have to hold on if you want the toilet, Sally," He added. "We've got a dragon using ours." And with that he passed out.

The dragon was studying Sally with interest. She was a small human and he could probably cook her if he wished. Instead, the dragon coughed slightly and a brilliant red and gold flame shot out and travelled up the shower curtain.

"Well thank you very much!" said Sally rushing to turn the shower attachment on.

" Shower curtains don't grow on trees you know! They cost money!" She furiously doused the burning curtain in a jet of cold water. The dragon leapt up onto the side of the bath and eagerly lapped up any stray water with a long forked tongue. Sally had an idea and turned the nozzle on to the dragon. It delighted in getting soaked, flicking its tongue out wildly to get a good long drink. "You were quite thirsty weren't you?" she said turning the tap off. The small, blue shape gave a satisfied cough. A grey cloud of smoke escaped from its mouth.

Professor Mudgett woke up and pointed a finger feebly at the Dragon.

"Back, you beast!" he stuttered as he tried to stand.

Then, not really knowing what course of action to take, The Professor stood rooted to the spot. The small, blue dragon shuffled over towards his feet and gazed up at him, its yellow eyes opened wide.

"It's quite sweet really," muttered Professor Mudgett, feeling utterly ashamed. "It's almost like having an ugly, blue dog, with no fur."

The dragon's little, round head cocked to the side before it let out a weak and gentle flame that gently singed both Professor Mudgett's eyebrows.

"I think you asked for that, Dad," remarked his daughter.

CHAPTER 4

The Mighty King Poe was sitting on the roof of his restaurant scanning the skies with a pair of binoculars.

"Hello everyone," he rehearsed. "Welcome to my restaurant! Ladies and gentleman, if you would like to queue in an orderly fashion you will have a chance to sample my delicious Chinese cuisine and see the world famous Blue Dragon! Yes! I'm afraid that prices have gone up! But that is business! So step inside!"

"Boss!" said the chef coming up the steps "Who are you talking to?"

THE CHEF
(*Derek Scrunge*)

52

"That's none of your business!" snapped King Poe stroking his burnt moustache.

"Boss, you promised to get some more noodles, now we've run out. How can I cook Chinese food if I have no noodles?"

"Improvise! Like you always do!" was his Boss's reply.

"Improvise? How can I? Noodles are noodles and you won't even let me buy the ingredients to make them myself!"

The Mighty King Poe set his binoculars down on the roof and thought for a moment.

"I think noodles look like fried worms. Go into the dump out there and find some worms and fry them. The customers will thank us. Worms are full of protein! Now go!"

The chef sighed.

"How can I make Chinese food without real Chinese ingredients?" he thought.

"Soon there will be no rice left and what will he have me use then? Maggots?"

He knew that he had better not suggest that, just in case.

King Poe scanned the dump again for a sign of the small, blue beastie. He might have dreamt the whole thing. But it was so vivid! And the Mudgett's overgrown garden was still there in the morning so some of it must be true. But a blue dragon in a cage! What an idea! Just the ticket to pull in the crowds.

His eyes rested on the Mudgett's garden. A very silly man lived there and a very annoying little girl. How nice it would be to get rid of them as well. If he had the money he would buy a bulldozer and move all the rubbish on to their plot and then have enough space next to the restaurant to build a big car park for all the expensive cars he would own. He'd get rid of that burnt old shed and that stupid, revolting house with its silly doors and windows. Especially that window of theirs, that looked out onto the garden. What and ugly looking window it was with that idiotic looking blue dragon peering out of it.

"My dragon!" he cried. "So it wasn't a dream! It's in the Mudgett's house!" What it was doing there he didn't know, but he knew one thing. It was his dragon and he wanted it back.

The small, blue beastie was having a good sniff out of the window. There were all sorts of interesting odours that it wanted to investigate out there. Its little, blue nostrils quivered with excitement and he began to flap his magnificent wings.

"No, don't fly way!" Sally cried, "I might never get you back!"

The dragon blinked at her and jumped down from the toilet seat. Professor Mudgett was furiously scribbling away in his notebook. Every so often he would whip out his tape measure and measure the length of the dragon's tail or head.

"Well it doesn't seem to be growing anymore," he announced. "Which I suppose is just as well, otherwise he would be very difficult to keep in the house."

"I hope he doesn't try and fly away," said Sally, as she stroked its head. "He might get into all sorts of trouble. I'll put a jumper on him to cover his wings."

Professor Mudgett agreed. "Let's keep out of sight for a while. I want to keep all this under wraps until I make another batch of my fantastic formula!"

Sally scooped up the dragon in her arms and carried him downstairs into the kitchen where it was much warmer.

She was going to enjoy having something to look after that was smaller than her father. As she watched the dragon lovingly set fire to the biscuit tin, she thought about what would happen if her father's formula fell into the wrong hands.

She wondered about all the things that a bad person could use it for and what they could bring to life. Sally concluded that if Professor Mudgett were to make another pot of the amazing mixture she would not tell him about the cup of tea. She was sure that the tea was what gave the potion its power. Deciding to let him make the formula without this vital ingredient, Sally fed her little, blue friend a burnt biscuit.

Outside The Mighty King Poe called to the chef who was busy collecting worms from in and around the tip.

"You there! Chef!" he bellowed. "Come up here onto this roof and bring the wok cleaner with you."

The chef let out a deep dramatic sigh and muttered a few words under his breath.

THE WOK CLEANER

A few minutes later he appeared with the wok cleaner.

" What's happened to your moustache?" asked the wok cleaner. The chef gave him a quick kick.

"Just shut up and listen will you!" Commanded King Poe. "I have decided that you two will be my henchmen, which are evil bodyguards who do my dirty work."

"I do your dirty wok!" said the wok cleaner.

"Not my dirty wok!" cried King Poe. "I want you to do my dirty work not dirty wok! I want you to do the evil jobs that I tell you to!"

"But I am a chef and he is just a wok cleaner!"

"Actually," announced the wok cleaner, "I write romantic love poems when I am not at work cleaning woks."

"Really?" said the chef. "I would never have known..."

"Shut Up!" interrupted The Mighty King Poe.

"I want you two to start being mean and nasty and doing exactly what I tell you to! And before you two buffoons answer me back with words about cooking lovely Chinese dishes or composing silly, soppy love poems, listen to this! If you don't do as I say I will not only stop your wages but I won't pay you for all the previous weeks that I owe you!"

The chef and the wok cleaner froze when they heard this.

"Now listen," continued The Mighty King Poe. "I want you to go out and get something of mine from the house next door. It is small and blue and breathes fire, so wear some thick gloves."

"What is it, a dragon?" laughed the chef.

"Yes," roared The Mighty King Poe. "It's a dragon!"

"One moment" said the chef. He took the wok cleaner aside and whispered.

"Has the boss been drinking?"

"No," replied the wok cleaner "He never drinks. He doesn't like to spend the money!"

"Well then, my friend, I think he has lost his marbles! He thinks there is a blue dragon living in the house next door."

"What are you two whispering about?" yelled The Mighty King Poe, in a temper.

"Nothing Boss!"

"I have a plan so you two noodle heads won't have to do any thinking. I want you two pretend you are window cleaners and wash the Mudgett's windows.

"This way no one gets suspicious. By washing the Mudgett's

windows, not only will you be providing a service but also you can get a good look inside! Then, when the moment is right, you go in, grab the little monster and shove it in a sack and bring it to me!" The Mighty King Poe thought about doing and evil laugh then wisely decided against it.

"Hang on a minute! We're not paid to clean windows," said the wok cleaner.

"I'm paid to clean woks and he's paid to cook."

"May I remind you that I haven't yet paid you for anything! And if you ever want paying, you'd better do as I say! Now go! And don't forget! It breathes fire!"

Reluctantly, the chef and the wok cleaner set off to kidnap the dragon next door.

CHAPTER 5

Armed with a selection of cleaning equipment they arrived on the Mudgett's doorstep. The chef was just about to knock on the door when he looked down at the wok cleaner's bucket and spotted a toothbrush.

"You can't use your toothbrush to clean windows," said the chef. "It's not the right equipment! They will get suspicious and we won't have a chance to kidnap the dragon!"

"I'm not using my toothbrush!" retorted the wok cleaner.

"Well, what's that then?" asked the chef, pointing at the offending object.

"That's *your* toothbrush!" replied the wok cleaner.

Before the chef could take a swipe at his fellow henchman, Sally came to the door to see what the noise was.

"Who are you?" she asked eyeing them warily.

"We are window cleaners," said the chef.

"And we have come to clean your windows," chirped the wok cleaner.

"My dad cleans the windows here," Sally answered truthfully. "It saves money."

"Yes, but this is a free trial" said the chef nodding excessively.

"We are cleaning windows for all the houses in the vicinity, completely free of charge."

"There are no other houses round here and..." she became a little distrustful... "Why are you both wearing chefs' hats?" But before they could think of an answer the dragon gave a loud anxious snort from the room next door.

"What was that?" asked the wok cleaner. "It sounded hideous!"

"That was my dad" Sally said hurriedly. "He's got a cold and a sore throat."

"Well he won't to be out here cleaning windows then!" the chef said, triumphantly.

"Yes, all right, you can clean the windows, then please go," Sally said, shutting the door.

Anything to get rid of those two strange men!

Upstairs, Professor Mudgett had gone to his bedroom for a lie down. It had been all a bit too much. As long as the strange, blue thing downstairs didn't burn the house down he thought it might be alright to grab a quick nap and recharge his batteries. In the past hour he had made another batch of mixture, but had grown too tired to try it out. He had followed the words of his marvellous formula right down to the last letter but somehow it didn't have quite the same consistency that the last batch had. Why can't formulas be like recipes?

Opening the bedroom window, Professor Mudgett took a good look at his new glorious garden. What a lot had happened that day! Yes, a short nap would do him good. He drew the curtains and lay on his bed pulling the blue sleeping bag right over his head.

Downstairs, Sally and the mini monster had been playing some games. She discovered that the dragon was very fond of ham sandwiches, which he enjoyed toasting himself with a controlled flame. The sandwiches could be thrown in mid air and the dragon could have them evenly toasted before they landed in its mouth.

While the animal munched away, Sally watched as the strange new window cleaners propped the ladder outside and climbed up to the top. They waved at her through the window and she wondered if they had caught sight of her little companion.

When they had both got to the top the wok cleaner asked, "Chef, did you see the kid in the jumper?"

"Yes, I did!" said the chef, "Ugly looking kid alright! Bright blue with huge nostrils! And that tail!

"I dunno, I suppose it's the fashion," he said, shaking his head. "Now let's go get a dragon!"

Peering in through the Professor's bedroom curtains, the pair blinked into the darkness beyond. "There it is!" said the wok cleaner as he pointed to the large, blue shape lying on the bed.

"It's a lot bigger than I thought."

"Yeah," agreed the Chef. "I don't want to get on the wrong side of that! Let's pour some water over it first before putting it in the sack."

Just then the large, blue shape let out an almighty snore.

The two henchmen nearly jumped out of their skins and momentarily wobbled on top of the ladder.

" Come on, let's get this over and done with!" And with that they climbed in through the window.

Professor Mudgett was having a very strange dream. It was about a small blue dragon, which was slightly misshapen with one ear missing. Then he dreamt that someone poured a bucket of water on his head and put a sack over him just as someone poured a bucket of water over his head and put a sack over him.

"Let me go!" he shouted.

"A talking dragon eh! No wonder the boss wanted it so badly!"

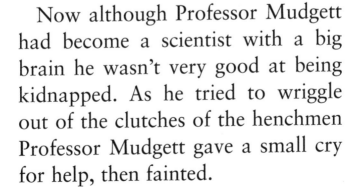

Now although Professor Mudgett had become a scientist with a big brain he wasn't very good at being kidnapped. As he tried to wriggle out of the clutches of the henchmen Professor Mudgett gave a small cry for help, then fainted.

The chef and the wok cleaner tied the end of the sack with string and dragged poor Professor Mudgett of the bed with a bumpty-bump. Then they hoisted him out through the window and the chef lifted him down the ladder like in a fireman's lift.

"Well" said the wok cleaner. "I think the boss is going to be extremely pleased with us, don't you?"

"We may even get a pay rise!"

As they descended the ladder, Sally began to question their window cleaning skills. She had noted that they had only cleaned one window and here they were marching off with a huge sack! How unprofessional! Thank goodness she hadn't given them a penny!

"Wait a minute," Sally thought. They had arrived with a sack that was empty and now they were leaving with a sack that was full. Something was in that sack, something that belonged to the Mudgett's house.

She rushed upstairs clutching the small, blue beastie under her arm. As she ran, it began shooting flames of excitement, but the panicked Sally had no time to put them out.

What had those window cleaners taken? She couldn't think. She rushed over to the bedroom window just in time to see the two men disappear into the restaurant next door carrying the large sack.

"Dad!" she called. "Dad! I think two men have taken something from the house!"

There was no answer. " Dad! Two window cleaners wearing chefs' hats! They've gone into the restaurant next door."

"They were carrying a sack shaped like you!"

Just then it struck her. But why would they steal her father?

But of course! The secret formula! Quick as lightening, Sally grabbed hold of the pot filled with the new batch of mixture and set off towards the restaurant with a fire breathing dragon under one arm and the little house which she shared with her father burning down behind her.

CHAPTER 6

The Mighty King Poe rubbed his hands together as he saw his not very evil henchmen drag the sack into the restaurant. As usual there were no customers that day, particularly as someone had spotted The Chef gathering worms from a rubbish tip.

"It's grown!" exclaimed a delighted King Poe as he eyed the heavy sack. " Put it in its cage. We can cut open the sack once it is safely locked inside."

The chef and the wok cleaner obeyed the command and dragged the sack inside the metal cage and slammed the door.

This woke Professor Mudgett with a start and he sat up rigid.

"Great! It's awake! Stand by with the water!"

The chef and the wok cleaner lifted two large buckets at the side of the metal cage.

As the bewildered Professor Mudgett struggled out of the sack the henchmen drenched him with the cold water.

"A dragon! A real dragon!" raved The Mighty King Poe as he strutted around the room. "This will bring the customers in! I won't even have to provide food!"

The chef tried to attract his boss's attention but there was no stopping the Mighty King Poe once in was in full flow.

"I'll charge a £100 to take a look at my blue dragon! I will be rich and famous! Everyone will know the name of The Mighty King Poe and his famous Chinese restaurant!" And it was at this point that he thought it would be appropriate to do an evil laugh.

He stopped halfway through his evil laugh when he saw the startled face of Professor Mudgett as he wriggled out of the sack clutching a blue sleeping bag.

"What is this?" he roared.

"It's a man," remarked the wok cleaner, somewhat amazed.

"I know it's a man! What's more, it's that idiot from next door! I asked for the blue dragon! I can't charge people £100 to look at a man in a sleeping bag! Where is the dragon?"

Suddenly the door burst open and Sally stormed in carrying a pot in one hand and the dragon under the other arm.

"I have what you want! Just let my Dad go!"

"Thank goodness for that! Hand it over then, small fry! Else your dad gets it."

"Gets what?" whimpered poor Professor Mudgett, nervously, from inside the cage.

"Cardboard pancakes filled with shredded wheat and gravy!" chirped the wok cleaner.

"Shut up you two!" growled The Mighty King Poe. "Come on, little girl, give me the dragon!"

"The dragon?" Sally queried. "What could you possibly want with the dragon?"

It wriggled under her arm and burped an appreciative flame.

"Of course I want the dragon! It's part of my clever and evil plan to make money."

"To make money?" Sally queried again. "Well that doesn't sound very clever and evil to me. No I thought the best clever and evil plans were to take over the world. Obviously I've been reading the wrong books!"

"Alright, alright!" growled The Mighty King Poe. "Give me a chance! I have to start somewhere!"

"Well you had a bit of practice when you stole our restaurant."

The Professor moaned from inside the cage.

"You see," Sally continued, putting the dragon and the pot of formula on the ground "You have to think big if you want to get anywhere in life. Now if I were planning to take over the world, Oh no, it's a silly idea…"

" Go on!" shouted The Mighty King Poe, sounding very interested and impressed. "Well! What would you do?"

"Well it's just that my dad has invented this amazing concoction that can bring anything to life. Well, just look at our garden fence and this little dragon here for proof. This time yesterday, before it came in contact with the potion, it was nothing but a lump of stone. Sorry," she said turning to the little, blue shape. "But you were."

"So?" interrupted King Poe, folding his arms.

"So! If it can bring things to life, which weren't alive before, just think what it would do to something that was already alive?" Sally drew a deep breath. "Just think what it would do to a human being! It would make them super human! With super human strengths and powers!"

This was a very bold statement for a little girl to make. But of course Sally knew that the new batch did not contain the vital ingredient of the first. It did not have a mug of tea floating in it.

The Mighty King Poe was intrigued. This annoying little pipsqueak seemed to know an awful lot about being evil and clever.

" Hmmm! Special powers you say! Let me test it out on the wok cleaner before I use it!"

"No!" Sally cried. "There is only enough formula to coat one person.

Only one person in this room can become a super human!"

"I could make another batch," said Professor Mudgett, unhelpfully.

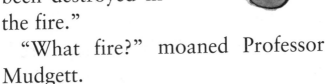

"I'm afraid you can't, Dad", Sally said, turning round to face her father. "All your scientific notes have been destroyed in the fire."

"What fire?" moaned Professor Mudgett.

"Our little, blue friend got very excited and started to burn everything just as we left the house, which explains why I have come here to bargain with the fat man with the moustache."

"My name, young lady, is The Mighty King Poe!" announced the fat man with the moustache.

"I heard a rumour it was Derek Scrunge," whispered the wok cleaner to his friend.

But Sally persisted. "The bargain I want to make with you is this. If you release my father and give us back our restaurant, I'll keep the dragon and employ these two men. Now doesn't that seem fair?"

"No it doesn't seem fair!" wailed King Poe.

"Oh yes," Sally remembered. "You can have this incredible formula in return."

"And if I do not agree?"

" If you do not agree, I will then simply tickle this dragon's tummy. He will then release a torrent of the hottest flames imaginable and burn the whole place down!"

"Burn the whole place down, you say? No I don't like that idea, that doesn't feature in my plan to become clever and evil, but becoming a super-duper human? Well that sounds most satisfactory!" said King Poe "Now give me the formula!"

As he stretched out a large fat hand towards the pot, Professor Mudgett cried out, "Stop! I don't think you should do that!"

But, of course, the fat man with the moustache was not about to listen to wise words of caution.

In his desire to be a super human and have extraordinary strengths and powers, The Mighty King Poe picked up the tub of mixture and poured the whole lot over his head. He then rubbed it all in, making sure he was completely covered from head to foot, taking special care to coat his moustache.

"Too late, little girl!" he trumpeted.

"When I become 'Super Poo, I mean Poe, I will take what I want anyway! The restaurant, the dragon and your father will be mine. Actually you can keep the last one. With my special powers, no one will stop me!"

It was at this point he felt a strange tingling sensation in his right foot, then his left.

"I can feel it! I can feel it working already! Any minute now I will have special powers!"

But before he could utter another word his face had solidified and his features had set rock hard. The pale liquid travelled down The Mighty King Poe's body until he was as stiff as a floorboard.

The large fat man with the moustache had become a large fat statue with a moustache.

"Is he dead?" asked the chef in a casual tone.

"No, not really," said Sally. "This sort of thing happens all the time when people want to take over the world. They usually come to a very sticky end. He has simply turned to stone. I think he makes a very unusual art work."

"Well I wouldn't want it in my front room" piped the wok cleaner. "Come on chef, we've got to look for new employment."

"There's no need for that," said the little girl as she released her father from his prison.

"I think that we could make this restaurant the best Chinese restaurant in town with help from the both of you."

"With real food?" asked the delighted chef.

"Real food" replied Sally scooping up the little, blue dragon in her arms. " Just delicious Chinese food and no gimmicks - oh except for a life size blue statue of a fat man with a burnt moustache."

"I love the food here, Anne" said one customer to another.

"So do I," said her friend "It's my favourite restaurant!"

" 'Flame grilled for extra flavour!' it says on the menu. Mind you, I think they have got trouble with their equipment."

"How do you mean, Maureen?" asked her friend, as she chomped on a succulent pork rib.

"They're forever calling out the fire brigade!"

"Well I wish they'd get rid of that sculpture. I like novelty, don't get me wrong, but it's enough to put you off your grilled dumplings! Can you come here please, waitress!"

"Actually I'm the manager," Sally said as she approached the women, "How may I help you ladies?"

"I don't suppose you could do something about that statue could you? Its eyes seem to follow you all around the restaurant! It's giving me and my friend here the creeps!"

"Yes, certainly," Sally replied throwing a tablecloth over the Mighty King Poe. "Is that better?"

"Much better, thank you."

As a smiling Sally walked towards another table, Anne leaned over and whispered to her friend.

"Ere! Last week my husband came out of this restaurant and swore he saw a dragon, flying overhead! I said to him, 'That's the last time you have a whole bottle of wine to yourself!' Honestly! A dragon!"

SALLY MUDGETT

MUDGETT'S
NEW HOUSE

MUDGETT'S
GARDEN

For David
S.C.

For my Dad with love
E.P.

First published in 2005
by Meadowside Children's Books
185 Fleet Street, London, EC4A 2HS

Text © Susan Chandler
Illlustrations © Emma Parrish 2005

The rights of Susan Chandler and Emma Parrish to be identified
as the author and illustrator of this work have been asserted
by them in accordance with the Copyright,
Designs and Patents Act, 1988

A CIP catalogue record for this book
is available from the British Library
Printed and bound in England by William Clowes Ltd, Beccles, Suffolk

10 9 8 7 6 5 4 3 2 1